To my beloved Eve;

Letters from Adam to his Wife

FRANCIS TESTA

PRODUCTIONS

To my Beloved Eve..."
Letters from Adam to his Wife

Dear Reader,

Everybody has an idea for a "Paradise." It's usually some mystical place where one can escape the so-called "real" world and most would prefer to live there if they had the choice.

Perhaps not surprisingly, the notion of Paradise is found in almost every kind of religion, from the real ones to the shams. Each seems to have a recollection, a legend, or just a mere rumor about an age when things were perfect.

In that lost epoch, men and women would not wrestle for power, humans would not eat meat, animals would be nice to us and to each other, no mosquitoes would suck our blood, no diseases would ravage our bodies, and peace would reign over an exciting and dynamic world.

That may sound like a good election platform and cynics would say it is probably just that, a good sales pitch. Paradise never existed and never will. If you buy in, you will always be looking for 'Paradise lost' instead of dealing with reality.

The problem with that answer, however, is the definition of reality. One man's reality could be another man's dream, or vice versa. And often is.

I don't believe the notion or desire for Paradise will ever disappear for one simple reason – people like it.

They want Paradise to be everything they search for: freedom, a nice cottage by the lake or a house on the beach, health, security, pleasure, comfort. But something always happens to pop the bubble, as it did way back for the owners of the "real" Paradise.

In the traditional story, humanity was fooled or seduced into giving it up by a mysterious agent of evil hiding within a snake. Many religions hold out the promise of finding it again one day, which is another reason the search for Paradise will not go away any time soon.

One of the most famous stories about Paradise is in the Christian Bible, in the book of Genesis, chapter 2, which says a Garden of Delights (a.k.a. Eden or Paradise) really did exist and was the original world created for humanity.

The beginning of the end for biblical Eden starts when Satan, hiding within a serpent, tempts Eve, the first woman, into eating "the forbidden fruit."

That was the fruit of knowledge of good and evil that God told Adam not to eat and in turn Adam told Eve. She didn't listen to him, ate some and then gave some to Adam to eat. Only after Adam ate the forbidden fruit did all hell break loose, as it were.

The resulting punishment by God was humanity's expulsion from Eden... Paradise lost. The world we live in now, therefore, is actually a long way from "home."

I thought about this one day and certain questions popped into my head. Was Adam angry with God for being booted out of Eden? What did he say to Eve about it? Did he blame her? If he was a real man, of course he blamed her. And if she was a real woman, I'm sure she found a way to blame him but probably didn't say it to his face right away.

What would life have been like for them, knowing that they had just sold Paradise for a lousy piece of fruit?

And where did Paradise go? If Adam and Eve were only expelled, it must still be around somewhere.

If he really did exist, how did Adam experience the severe changes he surely underwent after being thrown out of the garden of delights? It must have been like walking away from a Hawaiian beach party right into a Minnesota snowstorm.

And what was the deal with the serpent, a.k.a. "Satan"? Did he know the secret of the forbidden fruit? Did Satan lie or was he telling the truth? Why was that particular fruit, the fruit of knowledge of good and evil, forbidden to Adam and Eve? Did God want them to stay dumb? Were they that dumb in the first place? Was Eve right to take it?

All these questions made for an interesting mental exercise the day I hammered my thumb instead of a nail.

I especially hated the idea that "this is the way it is" as the pain emanated from hand-to-brain. I refused to believe that there was no answer to the question, "Why is the world the way it is?" (It really hurt!)

After all, without a cause there is no effect.

Without smashing my thumb, I would feel no pain.

That is why I wrote this book. I wanted to know how and why things were the way they were, if only to convince myself that my thumb would not hurt forever. (It's scarred though.)

I decided that the only way to do it was to put myself, as much as possible, into the mind and heart of Adam as he pours his thoughts out to Eve. He may or may not be fictional but he is the only man who experienced the loss of a "true" Paradise, a world without evil, where clothing was not necessary, growing old and decrepit wouldn't happen, and where domination, fear, violence, pain, and death held no power whatsoever.

Adam was not alone, however. There was a woman.

Briefly, for those who have no idea who Adam and Eve are and for those who think they know the Christian Bible, there are two stories of creation in the Book of Genesis, which are chapters 1 and 2 of Genesis respectively.

The first chapter has the more commonly heard tale of God creating the world and everything in it in six days; that's the "creationist" story. On Day Six, man and woman are created together in the image of God and given the task of multiplying and subduing the earth.

There is no mention of any fruit they must eat or avoid. There is a clear though unspoken equality between man and woman; they are obviously meant to rule the world together.

The second story of creation, which is much older according to some biblical scholars, has the man, Adam, being created alone on an empty earth. Only after Eden and the animals have been created does God create the first woman, Adam's so-called "helpmate." She is called Eve and sequentially is the last creature made.

Any number of days could have passed between the creation of Adam and Eve. It could have been years, who knows?

What that means is that Adam was alone in Paradise for a time, and he never needed any help to stay there. He only needed the woman's help to get thrown out... just kidding. Adam wouldn't have lost Paradise without the help of Eve, the first woman, the one he later had children with, the woman he loved, and probably hated for a time and then loved again.

The story says that when God confronted Adam about eating the forbidden fruit, Adam complained to God, "It was the woman you put here with me!"

That sounds like a definite foreshadowing of the way things would be.

I'm sure it was a rough ride the first few years outside of the Garden of Eden but in her defense, I don't see in the story that Eve pinned Adam to the ground and force-fed him the forbidden fruit.

It didn't matter. His excuse failed and he and Eve were kicked out of Paradise and we've been looking to get back there ever since.

The perennial negative assessment of the second tale is that Adam would have done all kinds of great things if Eve hadn't screwed everything up. Of course that suits half the population of the world but it's simply not true, and there are a number of other reasons why Eve was necessary for many great things to happen, not just the obvious.

Many of those reasons Adam realizes as he writes his letters because hindsight is often 20-20. As it happens, Adam writes in English, which is convenient because I write in English.

What I liked most in the second account of creation is that the second story allows Adam to grow into his world before Eve arrives.

That "growing up" feels very human and to me, more realistic. I used that context for the background of my character because when Adam describes or tries to describe to Eve what he felt, saw, experienced via letters, it is easier to imagine a very real man on a very real earth, dealing with phenomena that are unique to his circumstances yet familiar to the human condition.

The second story would also give Adam a lot to talk about with Eve after her arrival, providing them opportunity to get to know each other while falling in love.

That's a romantic notion, I suppose, but if God made two beautiful mortals naked in a Paradise, it's more fun to imagine what it would be like.

On a final note, I want to say that I gained a lot of insight by writing this, not the least of which is a serene but definitely enthusiastic pride and gratitude at the presence of women on earth and in my own life, a profound respect for the wisdom of God, gratitude for the gift of life, and a great deal of skepticism towards serpents selling fruit.

I hope you enjoy reading my book as much as I did writing it.

Sincerely,

Francis Testa

Adam recalls his first moments of life

My dearest Eve,

You know that I love you more than I can even understand at times.

Over the years I have come to love you deeply and appreciate your presence here on earth in ways both physical and spiritual (despite the few times I may have secretly wished for my rib back!)

Words cannot describe everything I feel for you and yet I will never stop trying because you inspire me.

The morning you arrived from the hand of God was the beginning of an entirely new existence. Before you can understand what that means for me, let me tell you what it was like before we, that is, God and I, made you. (We can argue about that later.)

I'm trying hard to think back to when I existed alone on earth (those few days), and it's with a great satisfaction I do... let me rephrase that before I'm sleeping outside again. I did not know what you were, before you were, so I can't be judged for what I did not know, right? After all, I had no idea what to expect of the world I opened my eyes to see so many lifetimes ago.

I recall rather vividly the moment I awoke to life. That day, I opened my eyes and I was aware that I was alive. There is no other way to say how I knew, I just knew. There was nothing around me, yet I felt energy coursing through my body, as though preparing me for what was to come.

A fresh gust of wind blew into my face, circulated within me, right down to my feet and out through the top of my head, as if making sure every part of me was fully functioning. I blinked a few times and felt the motion of my eyelids though I didn't know what to call them at the time. I stood up and turned a complete circle, staring out at a landscape that stretched far off into the distance. I still have no idea where it ends.

The soil of the earth was red, like a late sunset. A little stream of water was close by and I saw some hills a long way off. But other than that, there was nothing around.

Then a voice spoke - a deep comforting voice (I know you've heard the Voice). It permeated the world around me without being lost in it, and I instantly knew that the Voice belonged to the one who had made all this. I also knew that He had just made me, though He never said that exactly.

Again, I just knew it.

He told me to begin walking and suddenly I realized that I could, so I did. The earth felt warm and gentle on my feet.

I looked down at them, watching them as though they were detached. Slowly but surely I felt more and more in command of my own motion and soon the sense of being an observer of my own limbs disappeared.

My toes sensed every particle and each sensation was exhilarating to me, making each step more enjoyable than the last. And the effect of walking made me feel very good – such a simple thing, I know, but at that time it was a revelation.

I began to laugh out loud for pure joy, and the sound of my own voice was startling and strangely comforting. I could speak!

I walked for quite a while, faster, then slower, then fast again. Then I began to run and felt the wind against my face and body – what a great feeling, Eve! I can feel it all again even though I am now older and life has taken turns I never, ever would have expected.

I kept running for quite some time, stopping now and then to breathe – the air was sweet like a breath of honey. Though not as strong as something eaten, I remember savoring each breath like a good meal. As sweet as it was, the only thing I can think of that ever smelled sweeter was you, Eve.

But I'm getting ahead of myself.

As I was saying, I was too busy running, breathing, laughing and enjoying the energy that surged through me to think for a while. The little water I remember made for a great time as I splashed in it. I ran through one pool, enjoyed it so much that I turned around and ran back through it. I remember getting hit in the face with some water I kicked up – it tasted funny.

I bent down and saw myself then – that was a very strange moment. I was very pleasing to behold, I thought. I'm a man – man? Why did I know I was a man? I don't know, but I did.

I got tired of looking at myself – no, I was not there a long time – and decided to keep moving.

After more walking and running, I stopped to look around. That's when it occurred to me that I was probably in the same spot I had left but I couldn't tell. There was nothing different about the entire face of the earth from where I stood.

I looked up at that point and noticed the sky was so blue I was overcome with awe. It was much bluer that it is today, I don't know why that is. But in the glorious days of Eden, every color was so much more intense.

Red earth and blue sky and a globe of a sun – it never use to hurt my eyes at all. I could look right at it but never did it leave spots or cause me to look away.

Then I saw some clouds; long, streaking clouds that undulated like water. They were very white – that's all I remember thinking.

All the colors I saw were sparkling, deep, brilliant, and as I drew another breath I was very happy to be alive. Thinking back on it now,

I believe I would have sat there for days and enjoyed myself. But I'm glad now that God didn't make me do that. I felt there had to be more even if I would not have been able to say why.

Maybe God knew there was something I needed to find or somewhere unseen I needed to arrive to so I started walking again.

That's when it happened.

As I walked, beneath my very feet the earth began to change. Instead of red soil came green grass and I stopped moving. I was mesmerized by the changes happening right before my very eyes and beneath my feet! Trees began to rise from the earth, and flowers, and rocks... I was stunned but not frightened, never did I fear at all.

I felt the shaking of the earth as it opened to give up its beauty. I saw branches unfolding from tree trunks, heard the wind blowing and the leaves rustling. It was beyond anything you've ever seen or heard, except the birth of our children perhaps.

And the colors – Eve! I nearly fell over from the beauty!

Red, green, purple, pink, black, orange – and others I couldn't describe but you did after you arrived: fuchsia? I still don't know what that is... The flowers, trees, and fruit – all of it was completely breathtaking.

I remember the water pouring out from the earth into streams that flowed in among the trees and flowers. It sparkled in the sun, blue and green and clear as the sky – and all of it happening as I stood there and watched.

It was overwhelming and happening so fast it was difficult to keep up. I turned and turned, trying hard to see all of it. It was so fantastic I wanted it to slow down so I could enjoy it... and then the earth shook again and mountains formed, far away, but still I could feel it.

Eve, you must believe me when I tell you that nothing can replace those first moments of creation. I know you wanted to see it too but you'll have to try and understand what I understand now; it was supposed to be like this for you and for me so that we could learn to trust each other, and God.

I'm getting ahead of myself again.

While I marveled at the incredible world that just formed around me, the Voice said, "This is your home, Adam."

My home... and my name: Adam.

The words sent waves of confidence through me. I was breathless and excited and amazed and everything you can imagine, my love.

The Voice spoke to me again, telling me that here I was to live and to take care of the 'garden.' So I began to think of this as my garden, even though it was so big I don't think I or we ever found the edge of it while we lived there.

I miss those days, Eve. I wish I could have them back. Especially the short few we had together in Paradise.

Your loving husband,

Adam

To my Beloved Eve . . .

Adam's first day without Eve

My dearest Eve,

I love to watch the children laugh and play.

They have no concern for anything except where that little butterfly is going or what the animals are doing. For a short time at least they enjoy the freedom of a life without fear in their curiosity and I like that. It reminds me of those few days we had in the garden and how curious we were then.

Before your arrival I explored as much as possible, but I stopped so often I didn't get very far. There was simply too much to take in; the variety of flowers and trees, the water that poured out of the earth and over the rocks, down into the lagoon and out to the great river that flowed into the valley of lights.

All of it combined to make for an almost inconceivable variety of fascinating things, as well as the array of beauty - and all that even before the animals were made!

I distinctly remember feeling a profound inner peace that went all the way down to the bottom of my being – something I miss now in this world of constant threats and painful surprises.

In the garden, there was energy to life that made standing still seem like a waste of time... Time?

Time was not a factor in Paradise. It just occurred to me that I never thought about time at all in Eden, until we lost it.

Days, nights, mornings, evenings... it was like time did not exist, though I was aware of a 'before and after' to things I learned about. Maybe because time wasn't associated with hardship or suffering or death, it never occurred to me that hours were passing by or that time was a measure of my life.

Where was I? Oh yes, exploring.

There is a word I associate now more that ever about the beginning of the world for me. That word is "fearless."

I was completely unafraid and full of confidence about my life in Paradise like the children are before they see evil and death. In Eden, my curiosity drove me to discover all I could about the home provided for me.

The energy of life made me feel like I could run for a thousand days, and that is pretty much what I did, too. Running around had its benefits. That's how I found the meadow where we slept your first night in the garden.

There was a hill near the middle of the garden and I climbed to the top of it because the trees up there were so colorful. It also appeared to be the source of the stream pouring down over some rocks, near that lagoon we used to swim in. That is also how I found a lake up there and while not very big it was wonderfully blue and warm.

I remember I had to move a few branches out of the way to make a clearing. Only after breaking some off, throwing them into the stream, and watching them float away did I get the idea of pushing a tree over the stream to stand on top of it it.

I didn't manage very well. It was harder to push a tree over than I expected. In the process of trying, however, I learned the strength of my own body, which felt good.

My confidence grew even more.

You said yourself, Eve, that I don't notice small details and you're probably right. The trees were big, though, and I climbed a few while looking for one to push over. The sights from the upper branches were great, which is why I liked living on top of the hill I suppose.

That night, after a long day of exploring, I stood on the crest of the hill and looked out over the world..., my world, made before my eyes and given to me to care for. It seemed bigger all the time, but that felt like a challenge to me and I liked it. I still didn't know what exactly I would do with it all by myself.

It is strange to think back on that moment. You have to remember that there were no animals and no birds yet; no one, except God whom I could not see but somehow felt He was around, and me.

You might wonder why I didn't ask God if there would be any more people like me. It's because I had no sense of being alone.

Every sound I heard, every sensation I felt moving through me strengthened my sense of belonging from moment to moment.

The possibilities were endless, Eve!

I really wanted to build things. I hadn't really built anything yet but I was enjoying using my strength to rearrange things to my liking. I did build a few bridges there and you used them from time to time.

I remember how God came by to see me and asked how I was enjoying my home. I told him it was wonderful and that I wanted to build something but I didn't know what yet. All He said was,, "'Very good'," which was enough to make me feel great inside.

For some mysterious reason what I was doing was "'very good'" and I couldn't wait to do it all again tomorrow!

I lay down that night and looked up at the stars – countless, sparkling, mesmerizing, and much like they are now. That's another thing I know we still have from Paradise.

The stars were sparkling white, and some were red and, green while others appeared to be flying.

Bright as they were, however, the moon was brighter. It was very close to the earth that first night and the moonlight cast a blue glow over everything. (I loved how your body glowed under the moonlight.)

If I had felt a challenge from the size of the earth, space offered yet another even greater mystery to our life I still cannot fully grasp, my love. The vast darkness, punctuated by millions of tiny stars, took my breath away and still does. I know how you love it.

Before I closed my eyes to sleep, I remember thinking that tomorrow I would find a way to push a tree over into the water. I never got around to it. The next day God would suggest I needed a helpmate.

As I write this, I'm starting to think maybe that wasn't a coincidence.

Your loving husband,

Adam

God and Adam go in "search" of a helpmate

My beloved Eve,

This morning while Abel was 'helping' you to pick fruit (which was very funny because he sampled much more than ended up in your basket), I was reminded of the search for you, my helpmate.

I'll never forget the day God and I found you.

The morning of our search arrived with great promise. The sun appeared over the horizon, casting a warm orange glow over the landscape. A very gentle breeze blew through the leaves. It was quiet and I listened to the sound of the wind before rising.

I'd had a strange dream during the night. I dreamed I heard laughter and singing from within the trees. When I went in search of whoever was laughing, I couldn't get there fast enough to see who it was. I always just missed them – there were a few voices - and then they would laugh some more.

I awoke confused as to what the dream might mean but soon forgot about it (no comments please). It was my second day in Paradise and I was ready to make some new discoveries, so I planned out what I was going to do. I think I had already decided where I would go that day, to a section of the garden that was covered in a beautiful white blanket of snow.

I know I took you there once but on that day the stunning colors of the flowers stood out against the brilliant snow covering the ground – what a sight! The sun was warm but the snow was cool. It felt soft and smooth beneath my feet, very pleasant, and I ended up rolling in it to see how it would feel – you remember how I showed you, I'm sure.

You tried it once when I wasn't around – don't deny it, I saw you – and laughed as much as I did.

I lay there covered in snow for a while enjoying the strange coolness against my skin. That was before I decided it was time to eat. I got hungry, and noticed a fruit tree at the crest of the small hill that was also covered in snow. I ran up to the top, it wasn't that far, and took some of its fruit. On the way down I slipped and slid all the way to the bottom of the hill, where I hit a tree. That was a lot of fun, so I did it again.

I would not want to do that now but then pain didn't exist.

I only remember the bump and the enjoyment of the sliding. After a few times I decided it would be better to finish up landing in the water beyond the tree I used to stop myself. The water was warm and tasted good, too. I remember watching the snow melting from my body and finding that a most interesting sight.

Before I forget, there's something I wanted to mention about that hill where I ate the fruit. On the other side there was a view into a valley, overflowing with trees and meadows, and the air sparkled there as though angels were moving among the trees. At the time, I thought it was the most exquisitely designed part of the garden I had seen to that point.

That is where I was planning to go next when I started slipping and sliding in the snow and forgot about it for a while... no comments.

I went up the hill again and was again thinking of making my way down into the "valley of lights" – that's what I called it – when I heard the Voice. He said,

"It is not good for you to be alone. Come, let us find you a helpmate".

Alone? Helpmate? Those ideas had never occurred to me.

Up to that point I didn't consider myself alone at all. I was there, God was obviously there and that was enough, wasn't it? But once God had said I was alone, the idea soon took hold of me and slowly the garden began to feel very large and in some mysterious way... empty.

Alone. I had to agree, there was no one else around. No animals, no birds, no you... all of a sudden, I felt as though I needed the help of someone to care for this immense and incredible world that surrounded me.

That is when a very exciting idea came into my head. I realized that God wanted to make more like myself and I felt as though He wanted me to be ready. And I thought I was until I met you, Eve...I hope you laugh at that.

Before I could say or think another thought, the sky opened and a ray of brilliant purple light pierced the earth, sending soil spiraling into the air. From the spinning soil, two magnificent birds appeared and took flight! Eve, I know you've heard it all before but what an amazing sight!

Giant, beautiful eagles were immediately soaring above my head and when they landed at my feet, God told me to give them a name. Me? Give them a name?

Mysteriously they were waiting for me, those two magnificent birds – waiting for me to tell them what they were. "Eagle" was the only word I could think of, so I said it. It must have agreed with them because they turned and took flight again.

I wanted to follow them because I felt

certain that such magnificent creatures were going to help me do something. Come to think of it, I remember wondering what exactly they would help me to do.

I had never seen anything fly before and yet these giant winged birds moved with such effortless intent; I suppose they were already helping me to see the incredible power of God.

My confidence in our Maker grew immensely as I watched the birds fly around. Please don't be offended but I was so impressed and amazed, I honestly thought that nothing else was necessary.

Now I'm laughing at such a ridiculous thought, Eve.

Nothing else necessary? Necessary for what?

I had no idea what my helpmate was so why would I know what was necessary or unnecessary? Who would dare to say "enough!" except the One who started all this? But were they my... helpmates?

I watched the eagles glide upon the winds when more thoughts came to me: they cannot speak as I speak. They do not look as I do... and there are two of them, and only one of me.

No, they cannot be the ones for me. God never said that to me, Eve, I concluded it myself and I was right.

Naturally, I did not know that you and I would be able to make more like ourselves – had no idea in fact, as you well remember (although I didn't need to be told twice!)

Without saying it, I simply continued to expect something else from God and that day He made all the animals.

Not a moment was wasted, Eve. What was most impressive was the speed at which the animals began to materialize from the earth, from the soil of the garden. As quickly as God brought them forth from the earth, He would bring them to me and I would name them. I marveled for the quiet world I had lived in was suddenly becoming a land full of life and energy.

I thought we would run out of room for everything! Then I remembered the valley I had meant to go explore earlier on and realized there would be more than enough room. I watched as the animals walked off to where I'm not sure, but each new pair seemed to know where it belonged in the world.

And there I was, waiting and watching for my helpmate to appear, so that I would be a pair, too. It occurs to me right now as I write this letter that I understood I was incomplete without knowing why. I needed "help" and only God could deliver what I needed.

I can hear you laughing now, Eve, but in those moments, how could I have known anything about the plan of God? I had no idea what a world was supposed to look like or how many animals were necessary to 'help me' do whatever it was I had to do (remember God was supposedly looking for a helpmate for me that day!)

All day He made animals and I would name them. And every time they were unique; different sizes, shapes, skin color, feathers... all of them fascinating, vibrant, some more clever than others. It was incredible to behold and I was mesmerized by it all though deep down as the sun was setting, I was aching with desire to see my helpmate.

By that time I had completely forgotten what life was like when nothing else existed. All my expectations were now resting in a God who seemed to be making everything except my helpmate!

Near the end of the day, the sun was a golden orb of fiery beauty on the horizon. I knew it would be dark soon and we still had not found you, my love. Then there was a long pause but no further animals were made.

I waited for God to continue and when nothing happened, I said out loud that there was none like myself here.

Do you know what He said to me, Eve? He said, "We'll look again tomorrow."

Tomorrow? Why not tonight? Can't we finish – there's time. Look, the sun still casts a light on the earth and I am not tired. But He wouldn't answer me. You would think after all those amazing creatures rising from the earth, after an entire day of waiting, that He would finish.

But God knew what was He was doing.

He was making me wait for his final, and I
would say, the jewel of all creation. And she
would be my helpmate... tomorrow.

Your loving husband,

Adam

Adam remembers the morning of Eve's creation

My dearest Eve,

I want to tell you about the morning I woke up to see you.

You see, the night before your arrival, I was very ambivalent. I thought that somehow I'd be stuck with the animals for a very long time while God tried to figure out what exactly my helpmate was going to be. Deep down I wondered how that could be possible.

After a day of making animals, I had figured out that since there were pairs of animals that looked the same, I expected someone that looked like me or close. And if I knew that, He had to know.

I didn't want to question Him – I had already mentioned that from among all the animals, there was none like myself. (Of course we weren't looking for an animal but a human.) But He had told me we would look again tomorrow.

Tomorrow.

I'm laughing now, but at that time tomorrow seemed like a long way away and I didn't want to wait that long. What choice did I have, though?

If I had known what a woman was and what beauty you would possess, my love, I'm sure I would never have slept that night!

As I lay down to sleep, I hoped that the next day would be better than today. That was a strange thought even to me, because I lived in Paradise and the world was so amazing to me, how could I be disappointed?

Before I could consider an answer to that unspoken question, sleep overcame me and I dreamt about your creation.

In my dream, there was a mysterious man of light but I couldn't see a face. I say 'man' because he was large, huge actually, and emanated light. In fact, he seemed to be composed of light but it also emanated from him so that he didn't seem to be like me... limited or confined to the 'body' he was in.

I knew it was our Maker because there was someone there but not anyone I could say that 'this is...' someone, do you understand? I don't know else to describe it.

In any case, this Man of Light reached into my side and took a piece of me – that was a bizarre feeling! I know He took something and it looked like a rib yet at the same time, I felt that my heart was expanded and suddenly larger, as though I had been given something, too.

That doesn't make any sense: someone takes something from you and yet you feel that you have more than before that moment. But that's how it was, Eve.

He took my rib and began to mold and shape it. And the shape was beautiful.

If you can hold your breath while sleeping, I was doing that.

I don't know how I knew it but I knew He was making my helpmate. His 'hands' molded and sculpted every part of you – and the curves of your body made me try and get a better look. But then the Man of Light stood in such a way that I couldn't see very well what He was making.

I tried to move around him but He just blocked my view. I started to get frustrated and yelled out, 'I want to see!'

Can you imagine that, Eve? I was shouting at God to let me see what He was doing. I had seen everything else, or so I thought, but you, He kept hidden. As soon as I had shouted I was afraid that he'd be angry but He never even turned around. I think I heard him laughing at me...a gentle laugh that made me feel silly but happy, like I do with the kids.

Anyhow, I couldn't see...it...well, you, but I caught glimpses of you and each time I did, I got even more anxious about whatever the man of light was making. What I was able to see around our Maker was something curvy, delicate, but completely engulfed in light.

And the shape – your shape... I remember thinking "What is that thing? What's it going to do? Will it speak? It looks great!"

Then the man of light turned to me, blocking you completely, and He seemed to smile. I think I heard him ask me if I wanted to wake up now, and I couldn't say 'yes' fast enough. Whatever the man of light had made, I had to see it and right away! Then He disappeared and darkness came over me.

All I remember was opening my eyes to see sky and birds in the branches of the trees. I jumped up, completely and fully awake, ready to see whatever He had made. And there was nothing-nothing-at least where I thought you should have been.

Only when I noticed the animals looking at something behind me did I turn around and see you – and then I couldn't breathe. Not for a moment or two. The overwhelming joy and feeling of completeness came over me and I said what I did – you remember, right? I couldn't think of anything else at the time.

Of all the things I had seen up to that moment, Eve, nothing compared to you.

Light, sun, the singing of the birds, the amazing animals He made... all of it seemed but a beautiful window frame through which to see you, the jewel of all creation. And all you could do is stare at me with those luminous blue eyes and not say a word.

I don't think I stopped talking for a while - was I really talking so much? I suppose I was. I wanted you to know all about the world you were now in, how it came to be, how you arrived after everything was completed... only now do I realize that nothing was really completed until you were made because without you, the doorway to new life would never be opened.

When you finally spoke and asked me my name, my brain froze. My name? Oh yes... Adam. Then you smiled, repeated it, and I loved you forever.

Now we live in a world where evil and suffering are closer to us than the joy of Paradise.

But as long as you love me, Eve, and stay away from strange serpents, I can look into your eyes and know that even though we don't live there anymore, the best part of Paradise is still in the world.

Your loving husband,

Adam

Eve gets some new clothes

My dearest Eve,

I didn't mean to offend you today with that (little) comment I made about your new clothes.

All I said was that they didn't make you look thin – and you got so angry! When I started to laugh I saw a smile cross your lips but you didn't want me to see it so you threw a bowl at me.

You know I think you are more beautiful than the angels you talk about, it doesn't matter what you have on.

When you think about it, if we were still in Paradise... you wouldn't have missed.

With love,

Adam

Adam insists on remembering Paradise

My beloved Eve,

You know I feel very strongly about remembering those all too brief days in the garden.

The memory of Paradise keeps fear and sadness at bay and reminds us that we were made for a far better life than the one we are living now. The hope of a return to our real home is never far from my heart.

After Abel's body was buried in the earth, the promise of going home to God was whispered into my soul. Your dream about Abel telling you not to be sad anymore because he is at peace brought a secret joy to my soul that no serpent will ever steal away.

Without a doubt, this world we now inhabit is a shadowy reflection of the one planned and built for us by God.

It's true that we do not suffer every day. Indeed there are many happy moments with you and the children to remind me that we are not forgotten. But in Eden, it was infinitely better. We had only one enemy and he didn't conquer us as much as we defeated ourselves because of our lack of humility.

Now we have to relearn every day to trust and love one another, as well as fight off the many troubles that plague our existence since the exile.

At times you make me very angry and frustrated. Your ability to find my very soul and prick it with words leaves me speechless with rage. However, I refuse to bow to the will of the serpent and strike you for violence is the way of darkness. Could I strike the mother of my children, indeed, the mother of all the living?

There was a time I did want to leave you, to go in search of a world without a woman to cause me grief. I suppose similar feelings have arisen in you with respect to me, but the question remains – where would we go?

We were made for each other and together, with the hand of God most assuredly helping us, we've overcome many obstacles. I'm proud of those moments when we triumph, actually. It makes the days of peace all the more satisfying.

In those moments of frustration, however, I've heard the voice of the serpent whispering his desire:

"This is all her fault; she is the one who wanted to know evil."

You didn't want to know evil. You just thought you could get something denied us without asking for it and it didn't work.

How many times have I told the children to do as they're told because one day they'll understand? We took our time learning that simple truth.

I believe we both know that Paradise was the world we had first, the place of freedom and joy that was our gift, and our bodies are a constant reminder that within us we carry the wound of our lack of gratitude for what we had. Only now, because we have lost so much, are we aware of what we had.

Do you remember back in Eden, the morning you went off exploring while I slept? I do.

We had only been together one day and two nights and I woke up to find you gone. I actually felt my side to see if my rib was back – no, I didn't. I was certain God had not changed His mind. I knew you had gone exploring because the animals that normally stayed with us weren't there either.

I enjoyed my search for you that morning because I knew I would find you.

I still believe to this day that you heard me calling out to you but you were hiding and didn't respond…you did a rather good job of acting surprised when I found you. The memory still makes me laugh and I liked finding you, too.

How different it is now.

When you go out to bathe or you and the children go in search of things to cook for us, I worry about you until you return.

When Abel did not return home for the evening meal and Cain would not sit with us...the search for Abel was filled with dread for I knew there was something wrong.

It doesn't matter how hard I try, Eve, I cannot avoid comparing the complete freedom from evil we enjoyed in Eden from the constant vigilance we must now keep to avoid harm. If only we had learned to value what we had before we lost it, then perhaps Cain would not have killed his brother and we would still be living in Eden.

I hope the rest of the children learn the lesson we did not. Who knows? Maybe God in His providence will reward us with a passage back to Paradise one day.

Your loving husband,

Adam

The days with Eve in Paradise

My beloved Eve,

I know you don't mind hearing about what I thought of you in Paradise, especially the day you were born to life.

You were so unimaginably beautiful in every way; I couldn't take my eyes off you... I awoke from my dream and jumped up – I know, I was looking the wrong way at first and didn't even see you. Every time you tell the story to the children, you laugh as much as they do.

Let me state once again it was because, in my dream, you were standing at my feet not behind my head. God obviously has a sense of humor. I have to admit it was even more exciting when I finally did turn around to see that you were truly alive – and how!

My eyes must have bulged out because I remember your own amazed expression when we beheld each other. My heart began pounding with excitement at your presence. I think I had just learned again how fantastic the world of Eden was.

I've been trying to find the right way to describe what was so particularly important about that moment and now I know what it was; it was like the first moments of my own awakening.

In you I saw a vision of living beauty that completely changed my way of seeing the world. I knew to my innermost being that you were a woman, the helpmate, the one necessary for me. And your creation was completely beyond anything I had imagined or ever could have.

One thing I felt with absolute certainty was that God was proud of you, Eve. He was proud of His handiwork and who can fault him, except Satan?

As certain as I am of the earth beneath my feet, I am fully convinced that God knew exactly what He was doing when He made you - and well before He told me I needed a helpmate. I blurted out the first things that came into my head and later on you would ask me if I really did feel it when God took a rib.

I still don't know if He really took one of my ribs or not, Eve. In my heart of hearts, I believe He took my desire to be with another, the same one He planted there as we "searched" for you, and pretended to use it in your creation.

Everything about you glowed as if you caught the rays of the morning sun and distributed them without effort.

Your long dark hair glistened and your blue eyes, so deep and inviting, simply sparkled. The curves of your body were most pleasing to my eye, and still are. Your skin was so smooth the light caressed it like a gentle breeze and when you walked, you moved with such graceful motion such that not even among the giant cats could you find a rival.

You were like me but definitely no man; your form so wonderfully balanced and your radiance so soothing to my eyes, only a God who feared nothing could bring you to life, my love.

I compare you now to what you were then and I conclude that you were like a window into something I couldn't see except you did not impede the view – you were the view and the viewer and the window through which a glimpse of heaven was being sent from God.

Your beauty itself contained it and offered it to me in a manner I could enjoy without feeling oppressed by my own desires.

I'm reading my own words back to me and they sound almost too ridiculous and wonderful, perhaps even unfair to write especially now that we have lost Paradise and the grace of its freedom. But it's all true and because it is real to me and to God who made you, it is honest.

Eden is where you are from, Eve. It is your proper home, the one prepared for you before you stood on the earth and changed it, and me, forever.

I remember with some pain that there was nothing impure about my gaze then and nothing to be ashamed of for you or me. I feel now as though you must be careful how I gaze upon you. Certainly you sense the darkness that Satan has planted in the depths of my soul and somehow, in some strange manner, looks at you through my eyes.

His desires have nothing to do with love, however.

Somehow, displaying ourselves for the other is not something to be enjoyed like it was. Now intermingled with my love is an angry passion seeking to dominate you relentlessly. It is not at all like the passion that you stirred in me in Eden. That was a far sweeter passion to taste because it grew from love, not power.

There, you inspired me to great things and you would never have been ashamed or afraid to display yourself for my eyes. You took great pride in your beauty and despite your sin, God has not denied you the power to pass on your gifts of beauty and, I would now add, wisdom.

For that, I am very grateful. Your beauty will be passed down through all future generations just like it was meant to, even if it will one day know corruption. I only hope and pray that any gift we give our children will lead them back to Paradise and not into the darkness.

When I started to talk to you in Eden, you looked at me with a confused expression. I realized you didn't know anything at all about your surroundings – how could you? You had only just arrived. Thus I began to recount all I had seen up to your creation.

You stayed so close to me as I took you around to show you our home, I could smell the air around you – I couldn't breathe enough in! I'm glad you didn't notice... did you?... because I loved it.

At one point – and I remember it like it happened just now – you touched my arm to slow me down because you wanted to know my name. Your touch was light but it stopped me immediately because I enjoyed it and just wanted to do whatever it was that you wanted at that moment.

I told you my name and just hearing you say it brought a surge of confidence to me.

I meant to ask you why you waited so long to speak. I thought (and don't blame me, you were new) that you might not know how to speak... how foolish was that?

When you did finally speak, your voice was soft and your mouth shaped so exquisitely, it made your words appear in the air as though I could see them. I couldn't wait to hear more... at least in those days! It might have taken a couple of days but your questions certainly increased in frequency, and were good ones, I must say.

But that first night together you didn't say much except one thing; you said I was beautiful and that you liked to hear my voice.

I... beautiful... it felt so good I almost couldn't sleep.

You curled up and went to sleep shortly after and I marveled at your beauty, thinking, what is this amazing creature beside me? Am I to be with her all my days? That was the first time I ever thought about how long I would dwell in Paradise, and it was because I wanted to be sure you would be around.

You started me thinking about Eden in an entirely new way, about what I would build and how I would do it, and if you would like it.

The next day we went to all the places I had been before you arrived, and it was all new again because you saw things I never noticed before. I'd never seen any kind of fish, but you saw an entire school of them in the lake. I didn't know where they came from, and you named them for us.

You noticed the tiny animals that moved among the grass in the meadow, and they seemed to love you. The horses shook their manes and bowed to you like you were their mistress, and you laughed and looked at me with great satisfaction.

Yes, Paradise was definitely your home, too, my love. You grew in confidence, and dare I say, beauty, if that were possible.

I was so proud to have you with me then.

That night, the second of the three nights we spent in Paradise together, you asked me a question I did not know how to answer at all; what does it mean to die?

Now I know that it means we lose everything and must leave our bodies to return to the earth. If only we had asked God that question, perhaps you would have chosen to ignore the serpent and we would be enjoying Eden today.

No matter what, Eve, I will always be grateful that God gave you to me.

Your loving husband,

Adam

To my Beloved Eve...

Adam worries about Eve's sickness

My dearest Eve,

I write this to comfort myself more than you, I know, but I cannot help myself.

Your sickness will not abandon its evil intent and though you tell me not to fear, I worry that you might be taken away from me. I know it is not true to think God is angry but that does not comfort me now. I only want my wife to be well again.

I will go to the offering pyre to plead for your return to health. May God hear my prayers.

With great love,

Adam

Adam says God's law in Eden was good for he and Eve

My beloved Eve,

Today I must have told Abel to take the sheep down to the river at least ten times. By the tenth time I was yelling and he finally did it. I know he wasn't ignoring me. His head was elsewhere, that's all.

Somehow, I can't stay angry at him. His heart is full of the few things that bring joy in this world.

Not like Cain, who grows angrier each day and deliberately ignores me. With him I must almost threaten violence to get anything done. He blames me for the loss of Paradise, though he takes it out on you with his cutting remarks. There's no excuse for Cain to speak ill of you or to disrespect his mother without whom he would have no life at all.

I don't like it when you make excuses for him especially after I tell him to shut his mouth; you are still blaming yourself for the hardships the children suffer. Stop it, Eve. What's done is done and we must live with it. We were both there and we are both to blame for the state of our life.

We have put the dark days of our own fighting and blaming each other behind us in order to build a world that is as good as possible for ourselves and our children. I forgave you and you forgave me and that's that.

It's not like I'm telling him to do things that make him suffer undue hardships. I wonder if he would see what he has in a better light if it were all taken away from him. We certainly look back and see with piercing clarity what we have so heedlessly rejected.

I think back to Paradise where one law was our only limitation. There was no shame in being subjected to it, when everything we desired was laid at our feet. But in my heart I know it wasn't simply the fruit of the tree of knowledge we were forbidden to eat, was it, Eve?

No, that was merely the simple instrument God used to ask for our gratitude for His gifts.

The serpent spoke as though we would gain something we did not possess. For all the fruit of Eden, I cannot imagine what we did not have already, except one thing perhaps: humility. Where were we before we arrived on earth? Do you remember, my love?

Of course you don't because we did not make the world or ourselves.

Take for instance the clothes we need to cover our bodies. Why do we need them? It's not like we do not take the gift of our bodies at the opportune times. On the contrary, we are not denied the pleasure as though it were something we stole from Paradise, we did not. It came with our bodies and remains with us now.

That is a sure proof the law of God in Eden did not intend to stop us from being what we are as man and woman.

The shame we feel is because we have lost the veil of God that shielded us from the eyes of another who looks hungrily upon us now – you especially, my love. I feel in my soul that another covets it and most assuredly not the one who made it but the one who took the form of a serpent and pretended to be the keeper of secret knowledge.

Did you hear Cain and Abel fighting the other day? Cain demanded that Abel surrender a piece of his field for crops. When Abel refused, Cain shouted that it was "his property" to use and he would kill Abel's sheep if they did not stay off what he "owned." If I had not stepped between them and threatened to punish Cain, I don't know where it would have ended.

Cain drew a line on the ground and began to pile rocks up as if making a fence would grant him what he wanted. When I ordered him to take it down, he glared at me as though I were somehow an enemy to him. How did Cain come to possess his vision of the world?

Is that what we looked like to God on the day we ate the fruit? We drew a line and God respected our desires, foolish as they were.

I tell you this because it is not going to end with Cain. The disrespect, the anger, the desire to own another's possessions or kill another's animals – that will grow as surely as the very earth fights against us now outside of Eden.

Once we commanded the birds of the air and animals of the sea to obey. They flee from us now, or worse, threaten to use us as food. All because we did not want to accept God's only law, given to us for our own good.

Cain pushed his sister to the ground just the other day. I took a stick and hit him hard enough to make him recall his own weaknesses and then he fled from me. And so he should because his anger and my strength will come to blows if he does not learn to respect my authority or the women of his own blood.

What further violence awaits the women who have no one to protect them?

Eve, you ask me not to banish Cain because you think he will learn to value what he has. But at the same time, you warn me to watch him and Abel...I don't understand you sometimes. For the sake of his mother, I will not send him away. I must say that I have long sensed that he will turn his back and walk away from us and from the world we offer him.

Only God knows how and when. Perhaps I am wrong. If I am right, however, the world he will rule will be one of harsh and brutal laws and there will be no respect for the woman he shares it with.

He thinks he can force his way into Eden by conquering the angel that guards the entrance. I wish him strength. He has not seen the angel – a hundred men will not defeat it.

When I look at you, my love, I feel that somehow the law of God though given for both of us, was more for you than me. The way God made me wait for you to arrive, the body He gave to me and the body He gave to you, surely those are guardians of knowledge, too?

The law protected the knowledge we had for each other, not just from the dangers outside of Paradise.

What secrets were waiting to be discovered by us if we had turned from the forbidden fruit? Would another, even greater gift have been granted to us both? What did God want us to discover that will remain forever a mystery because we are no longer worthy of receiving it?

If I've learned anything at all from our life together so far, Eve, it is this: God's law was not in place to stop us but to direct us to where we would find what we wanted.

Pray Cain learns that lesson before it is too late for him.

Your loving husband,

Adam

Adam wonders at the mystery of Eve

My beloved Eve,

Do you remember that day in Eden you told me you were a mother? I certainly do.

I think I knew something exciting was going to happen that day. True, every day in Eden was an adventure but that day was unique. It was the second, no, third day – I can't remember now, of our life together in Paradise.

I recall that you had left me sleeping because you wanted to make some discoveries of your own. I admit that I enjoyed it when you found things that I had never seen. Your excitement made Eden seem even more mysterious. (It is possible, though I'm not admitting it, that I thought I had seen it all.)

In any case, I went searching for you and found you behind the waterfall, in that beautiful meadow where the little pool was. I can see you now, sitting up, flowers in your hair – you looked so wonderful I couldn't speak. You had laid out all kinds of fruit on the ground for me, but your expression was one of gentle confidence when you invited me over to sit down.

I sensed that you were different some-how but I was hungry and the vision of your beauty kept me silent, so I sat down and started to eat.

The memory of our conversation that morning always makes me laugh. You said some angels ("beautiful little angels" you called them) had appeared to you and called you the "doorway to life" for other men and women to come into the world. You were going to be the "mother of nations," they said.

Mother. A word so simple yet beyond my comprehension; what was a "mother"?

All I remember thinking at that moment was, "That's the last time I let her go exploring without me," and not because I didn't believe you. I never doubted that you believed what you said. I didn't know where or how such an amazing thing could be possible – other men and women entering the world through you?

Neither of us knew how to make a baby, as I recall. The day we did figure that out was a very pleasant surprise indeed, but "mother" or "father" didn't mean anything to me yet. The word "mother" only came to life for me on the day of Cain's birth.

The vision of a newborn child in your arms was even more amazing than the rising of Eden from the earth. Through that one event the entire mystery of creation showed itself to be within you, my love.

When I think back to when I first laid
eyes on you, I saw your beauty as
something for my own enjoyment, and it
is. I marveled at the delicate nature of your
body, the softness of your touch, the
sweetness of your voice.

But there's much more to you I realize
now, much, much more. Your arrival was a
complete surprise to me in every way, not
just because you were made from my rib
but because of what you were – a woman.

God let me think we were searching for a
helpmate but He knew what I needed, what
the world needed. It needed you. And that
was only the beginning! I had only been on
earth for a few days and you quickly followed.
It is obvious that in order to build the earth there
had to be, and there was meant to be, more.

Every time a new life comes from your body,
a new hope emerges in both of us for the future.

I would never have gone in search of
you, Eve; how could I know what to look
for and where would I go to find something
that did not exist? I gaze upon you now,
the desire of my heart, and I know that you
are one of God's great secrets. No, I never
could have imagined something as
marvelous as you.

We are one by our humanity but definitely
two by divine design, which always reminds
me, even now in this world, that you are an
act of God's creative wisdom, the other half
of the world's future.

There are times when I find myself
staring at you, watching you speak or move.
In my heart I ask God how so much beauty
can still be here, on this darkened earth?
Beyond your remarkable gift of bearing
children, you seem to know the hearts of
those you love and sometimes even the
mind of the evil one.

The only time you are mistaken is when
anger, insecurity, or vanity clouds your
vision. Then you do things, as you did in
Eden, that you regret later.

We are linked in the spirit even more so
than when we come together in one flesh.

My strength can be doubled with a
supportive word from your lips and cut in
half if you decide that I am unworthy of
your kindness. Secretly I am grateful that
you find more good than evil in my work
and tell me so. I have no reason to believe the
power of your words was not given to you
by God because I am helpless to fight it.

My only retreat from such power is to
hide in the fields and give myself to the task
of building a world Satan cannot destroy
with his cunning.

Sometimes I grow angry with you and
demand your silence. But the Lord rebukes
me if I am cruel for I am no less fallen from
where I once stood. The entire world was
beneath my feet when God first gave it to me,
before Satan showed me how to abandon
peace for violence.

Now, satisfaction can only be found in the shedding of blood, sweat, and tears and we both know what that means, especially you, Eve.

The serpent whispers that you must be controlled or you will destroy the world. He holds up Eden as proof but he lies. I am angry sometimes that you failed to expose him at the tree but I served his purpose willingly. I will not serve him anymore.

You must be alone with your thoughts and desires, too.

I do not wish to own you by the power of brutality. The very concept of owning you never entered my mind until the dawn of Evil and cannot be the will of God.

I have thought about this a lot, my love, because you never cease to fascinate me. You arrived on earth by the hand of God but did what you did by your own thought and will. Selfish though it was, it does not change the importance of your creation.

How could you be a true helpmate to me if you are not free? You are the Mother of all the Living and it would destroy the very purpose of your creation if I caged you as one of the animals.

If only we had turned from the serpent's lies I would never fear your tongue or the power you possess to see into my soul. We cannot see him anymore for he hides among us and inside of us – how I wish I could expel him from this earth!

It pains me to say it but I do not always

trust the words that come from your mouth. Are they from our Maker, or from our enemy? Are they born of love or do they spring from fear and anger? Did Satan not speak with you first after all?

In this hard existence I do not possess the absolute confidence in your word like I did in Paradise. Abel seems to understand the new order of life but Cain despises it. I think he did from the beginning – and he blames you the most. Your tears and frustration at being so cleverly manipulated by the serpent have taught you to turn to God first for answers now.

I am proud of you for being strong against his malice. You are the reason we hope, Eve.

Without you, what possibility could there be for the destruction of Satan? We all know, and God is my witness, I have faithfully reminded the children (and myself) of the promise that you received from Him; your seed will crush the serpent's head one day.

Today the youngest of our children played and helped me in the fields. I see you and me in them; my daughters have your beauty, my sons possess my strength. I love them all so deeply I cannot express it with words.

Even Cain, despite his self-indulgent anger, is my flesh and blood and I love him. I pray that he will find it in his heart to forgive us for our offense in Eden.

In all this I am only saying the truth; without you, my love, there would be no children in this world.

You bring forth life by strength I can only attribute to God and you. I know nothing of your pain, though I certainly hear your cries of anguish. I can only admire your powers with awe and with no shame I say that I am humbled by your gifts.

When you give birth, I am the most proud of you. If there is a moment Satan dreads it must be the birth of a new human being, for who can know if this is the one God sends to deliver us from evil?

I've come to realize and I think you will agree with me – that day in Eden when you told me you were a "mother"? That was the greatest knowledge – and you already possessed it.

With all my love,

Adam

Adam recalls the day Cain murdered Abel and the birth of Seth

My beloved Eve,

The sadness of death creeps towards my soul. I see it in your eyes, too. In a few days we will remember the death of Abel and mourn him once again.

Only now, after all these years, can I distinguish between the sorrow and anger I felt when I found our son's dead body.

You cried out to me when I ran off because you thought I went in search of Cain to kill him. I'm sorry I made you suffer even more in that moment, my love, but it couldn't be helped. I knew where Cain was - the Lord told me. Maybe I did want to exact revenge on him.

The truth is, I ran away from you because I saw the pain in your eyes, and felt the agony that pierced your heart. There was nothing I could do and I felt so useless I simply didn't have the strength to be near you.

Death separated me from you again , and I couldn't stop it. Not only was I torn with anguish, I was disgusted at myself.

The raging mix of anger and sorrow inside me screamed with frustration because Abel's death never had to happen.

When I first saw him there, lying on the ground, I didn't see the blood. I thought he slept, so I shook him and that's when I felt the coldness of his flesh and recoiled in shock. Understanding came slowly to me.

Then I saw the blood, so much I couldn't believe it... and the truth seized me with a darkness that poured into my mind and heart. All I could do was cry out.

Confusion, helplessness, deep sadness... all of those came at once, Eve.

I knew his spirit had left his body and the utter weakness I felt in the face of his death threatened to destroy me. I called out his name again and again as I held him close – as if that would do any good - pressing his face to my chest, feeling the blood on his head. I could even... smell it and it smelled like death.

Then blackness so profound permeated my soul, I felt like I was falling into a bottomless well. It was exactly like the moment I ate the forbidden fruit, only this time, it was Abel who died.

I screamed in anger then, cursing the day I brought death to the world. I cursed my life, my failures, and I cursed Cain. My own blood had killed his kin! I cried out to God for help but heard nothing. Evil had won again... I could not save Abel from its brutality.

Then you came running,; saw him there, and collapsed upon his body.

Abel was your favorite son. You never said so because you loved all your children, but we knew, Cain knew, and the evil one knew.

The voice of evil blamed you, Eve: "If she hadn't eaten the fruit," it said to me, "if she had only obeyed what you had told her about the tree, if God had never even made her, none of this would have happened. It's all her fault. She is the mistake!"

Shame covers me even now because I found myself agreeing at first. In my heart, I knew it was a lie but I couldn't resist him. What if you hadn't eaten the fruit? What if God had not created you at all? I would still be living in Paradise alive, yes... but alone.

And then, as if a window opened in my mind's eye, I could see you there, the morning you were created – like a shining star, promising great things to come! Light poured through you; everything about you seemed to make Eden, and me, better if that were possible.

Nothing about you was wrong, Eve.

No, the evil one was wrong. God did not make a mistake when He made you, my love. You and I make mistakes, but not Him.

Without you I could not have perceived the wonder of God, himself. He made you and you were nothing I could have imagined as a helpmate. Neither Cain nor Abel, nor any of our children with all the promises they bring, discovering things we had forgotten, fearless in their innocence despite not having been born in Paradise... none of them could ever have come into being without you.

Seeing your body shake with uncontrollable grief over Abel's corpse made me so angry with Cain, I wanted to strike him dead right there and then! He took away something you loved so much, he deserved to die. I held back from going in search of him – you heard me cry his name in rage. It was your eyes that drove me away; pools of sadness that looked to me for help and I could do nothing.

The shadow of death had covered Abel and now it wanted you, me, all of us. No, no, no... that's all I could say out loud to myself.

Alone in the woods where I hid from you that night, the anger left me but the sorrow did not. We could have prevented all of this; we could have crushed the serpent's head while we stood above the little beast – we could have beaten death!

Why didn't I listen to you? You warned me on more than one occasion to keep a close watch over Abel because you felt Cain was plotting something against him. I thought too little of your warnings. Why would he plot against his own kin? And what would he plot - to kill his own brother?

The idea seemed so preposterous that I threw it out of my head. It even frightened me to think that you could perceive such a danger, so I chose to ignore it.

Now, forever, that will be a shame to me.

I won't lie. Alone in the trees, I thought of ways to kill Cain - I wanted to kill him because he helped death and stabbed you to your heart. The hatred I felt for my firstborn son was like nothing I had ever experienced.

Battling within myself, I turned to God seeking an answer to my question: why did you let this happen? He answered gently but truthfully and said to me,

"It was not my will for death to enter the world, Adam."

I realized then that Cain was like his father; we had both served death and others would have to suffer for it.

Then I wept bitterly, my love; for Abel, for you, for our children, and for myself. The horrible magnitude of my own sin weighed down upon me and I could not move for many hours. If not for the Lord commanding me to return to you, I don't think I would have moved from there.

However, in the moment I returned and we embraced I felt hope again.

The days following were hard but you were strong and I drew strength from you. You tell me now that it was the same for you. I don't know how that could have been. I thought you saw through me; saw my fear of the future.

If you did, you ignored it and only said the right things. Your words meant so much to me: "We can't go back, so let's go forward."

Then, on the day of Seth's birth, you smiled and said God had given you a new son in place of Abel.

He also gave you a new husband.

With love,

Adam.

Adam's remorse over eating the forbidden fruit

My dearest Eve,

I've never said this before but now that you're sick, I want to make you feel better as much as I can. It's my only way of not feeling helpless against the curse of suffering.

I hate pain and suffering because I cannot stop them – not in myself, not in you, not in our children. It's a minor chastisement for throwing away the world God offered us originally, but it's still a great mystery to me how it comes about.

With these words, I want to try at least to relieve you of any possible pain from the guilt you still carry from that horrible day in Paradise.

I don't blame you for eating the forbidden fruit. I didn't make you eat it, and without a doubt, you wanted to know what secrets it would reveal, but I have since come to admit my own participation on that day of shame.

On the day of our death to God, and in some way to each other, I couldn't begin to imagine the consequences of discovering the truth about lies.

Maybe I should have told you what the real name of the tree was but I didn't because I could not understand what "knowledge of good and evil" meant nor why it should be denied to me. Did I care? What is it to be denied one tree among countless others overflowing with fruit? I thought you would see it that way, too.

Thus, on the day I took you to the Tree of Knowledge and told you about God's commandment, I warned you,

"Don't eat of the fruit of the tree in the middle of the garden, or even touch it, or we'll die."

All I thought was that there's nothing to concern us as long as we don't eat that fruit. The name of the tree, the tree of knowledge of good and evil, didn't seem all that important to me at the time, only the avoidance of its fruit.

If you (or I, for that matter) never touched it, there would be no inclination to eat it, either. And after all the children we've had, I know I was right at least on one level.

I told you what I did to make it clear to avoid that tree but maybe I should have been clearer. Would it have made any difference? Is there something about "do not touch or eat" that is unclear?

Yes, I suppose there is. It doesn't answer the question "why?"

Every day I ask myself did the knowledge we supposedly gained from trusting

Satan really bring us a greater insight or happiness than we possessed already?

Never would I have thought that "knowing good and evil," would be so utterly useless – we didn't need to know about evil.

Fear, hatred, anger, violence, frustration, pain, suffering - who wants to know about all those things? I can't think of any reason why we would be motivated to take and eat such anguish!

All I wanted was to understand and I'm sure we could have done that another way – in fact, I'm certain that God could have given us a thousand times the serpent's knowledge without ever needing to do what we did.

Oh, the thought of how stupid we were – how stupid I was. It makes me so mad I could kill! The memory of those moments will haunt me until I die.

Satan, the enemy of our bodies and happiness, the dweller of a darkness that captured Cain and murdered Abel. That liar told you we wouldn't die but he never told us what death was, did he? And if we didn't know what death was, how could we know what to expect or to recognize it when we saw it?

Eve, sometimes I'm furious that you didn't help me to resist. But deep down I know it wasn't you or God; I did what I did. I want to run away from the words but I have to admit the truth.

I sacrificed you to find out the secret of the forbidden fruit.

I can see you now... touching the fruit as if it were a dangerous animal, expecting something, anything to happen. When nothing did, you plucked the fruit from the tree. Neither of us could see anything except that you were breaking the law of God without apparent consequences.

You didn't eat of it immediately - you looked at me waiting for me to say something but I didn't.

After all these years, I realize how deeply you see into me, Eve. You knew I wanted you to keep going. Taking the fruit must have been exciting for you.

I saw your face redden, flushed with anticipation. Surely there would be more to learn, right? All you had to do was eat it...

Inside I could hear my own voice screaming at me to stop you, to tell you to drop the fruit before you ate it because that's what God actually said – "don't eat it, or you'll die." But I didn't, and you kept going because... you... me... we wanted to know what would happen, and you wanted to be first this time.

As you finished eating the piece of fruit you held in your hands, you looked at me in a way that said it all: the serpent is right. Look at me, Adam. Nothing has changed.

Empowered by your new knowledge that God's law can be broken, you took another piece of fruit and held it out to me.

I know now that I had to care for you first, but I didn't. What's even more stupid is that I didn't even care about myself enough to walk away from you and the forbidden fruit. Instead, what did I do? I took it.

Your disdainful expression crushed my confidence in God, causing doubt to pierce my heart. I'm not blaming you, Eve, just telling you what happened to me in that moment. I didn't know what to think except that you had broken the only command-ment we had, yet I could see nothing different.

Now it was my turn to prove if God was telling us the truth – so I ate some, too.

Then the most horrible feeling I have ever felt came over me like a roaring wave.

A well of darkness opened up within me and from it sprung a limitless bilge of vile disgust at my own body, and a bottomless pit of hatred and anger that was directed at you, Eve. It blamed you without mercy for everything wrong at that moment.

I felt dirty and… hated… and I looked at you for understanding, but you cried out in fear and ran away from me! My head felt like it was going to explode for the crushing waves of knowledge – knowledge of evil and hate and cruelty… filling my head all at once! It made me sick and disgusted at myself, and you, Eve, the once shiny crown of creation.

Remember when Cain murdered his brother?

That day we felt in our own souls the value of the "knowledge of evil." The blood that seeped into the ground, the cold flesh of Abel's body, the fear and shame behind the eyes of Cain when we caught him – they were the same eyes of the serpent who spoke to you! He knew you could have beaten him then, Eve – yes, you could have crushed the serpent's head at the tree in Paradise.

Instead you listened to him, and I listened to you, and we despised God as though He were the liar.

What illusion was there in happiness, in life, in Paradise, in love, in your beauty that once directed the very light that poured out of the heavens over the earth?

The only reason evil cannot crush us now is because God protects us from the darkness that hungers for our deaths. But we both know it is not far away – Cain taught us that with the selfish murder of his own brother.

Now we must share a world infected with the evil that we let in! It sees and hates us, especially you, Eve, the doorway through whom his destroyer will come.

I don't want you to think that you alone must bear the weight of this sin. It is clear to me now that I had to protect you and I didn't. And now I can't even though I want to.

I wish that sometimes I could forget about Paradise but that would steal away the hope we have for God's promise to be fulfilled through you. If that were to happen, life itself would be an even crueler existence than it is now.

It pains me to think that all I had to do was not eat a single piece of fruit. I could justify it a thousand ways like a little child, but I'm not going to try anymore.

I failed you, my love. Please forgive me.

Your loving husband,

Adam

Adam tries to understand
how evil entered the world

My dearest Eve,

What are we that we could have let such a thing as evil into our world?

Were we doorways for something that lived within us, helping to open our eyes to see clearly the things we now only see through shadows and tears? Did you learn anything you really wanted to know by turning away from God? Are you more like him now that you have eaten of the fruit of knowledge? Is our Maker the source of fear, anger, conflict, and jealousy?

I'm almost certain you have no misconception about what you are – you are not all-powerful like God. I know I'm not anymore the wiser for having put my faith in a serpent. That liar said our eyes would be opened but were our eyes closed to begin with?

Yes and no, I suppose, or there would not have been any temptation to eat the forbidden fruit.

We saw, touched, lived and knew the world of Eden was real. We breathed it in and drank a happiness and energy of life that can never be achieved again. The only temptation then was to know how it all came to be – to seize the power of God. How foolish was that?

Now Satan tempts us to believe that it was all a dream; to think that nothing existed before the world we're in now. And I want to tell the serpent to his face that he is lower than the sheep droppings.

We were there, Eve. Eden was real.

On the other hand, we did not understand why the tree of knowledge was placed before us or why we should be denied its fruit. When the serpent said we could be like gods and know good and evil, why was that attractive to us? Could we have really become like God, creators of worlds, knowing the "secrets" of Paradise... could all of that have been made possible by the eating of a piece of fruit?

That seems so foolish now it makes me laugh but we believed it, or wanted to believe it, and we judged God the cheat and the liar for keeping it from us. Not once did we stop to question the one mocking God's words with his own:

"Of course you will not die!" Is that so?

We should have asked him, "Who are you? Are you a god? How do you know we won't die? Do you know what death is? Did you make the garden, the world, the woman?"

He is no god. He would never have made you, Eve. And if he were a god or even a real rival to God, he would have killed you right there in the garden.

Think about it. When God returned that afternoon – where did He go? – He told the serpent that your seed would bring forth the one to kill him. If Satan were so powerful, he would have killed you right then and there but he cannot.

The serpent is a fraud. He is weak and needs men to kill other men the way Cain killed Abel. The darkness overcame our firstborn and carried him off into a world of anger and violence but God is more powerful than the darkness.

That truth makes me ask God everyday to protect you, my love, so that you will bring forth the seed of Satan's destruction and help us all to find Paradise again.

I have decided - for what other explanation can there be? – that we were already like God before we ate the fruit.

Certainly, we didn't know it at the time...that's why we wanted to possess the knowledge hidden in the fruit.

What we did know was that we were free in Eden, Eve. We had no need to suffer or to lose our lives to learn that we were free. From the great height of your freedom, you gazed down upon the serpent in fascination and wondered as to its origin, but you were not afraid of it.

You and I were masters over it. Not like now. Now the serpent has power.

He roams about like an uncaged beast, mysteriously moving in this world, through our bodies and minds – and all because we released him, Eve. I don't understand how it happened but I'll never forget the moment evil gouged a path through my soul leaving a wound that will not heal. It's as clear as the memory of the fall that left a scar on the back of my arm.

You feel the wounds too, don't you?

You've told me that at times you sense the eyes of something sinister watching you and I can understand why. Every time you give birth to a child who knows what wonderful potential lies with our son or daughter? You've told me many times that you are excited every day to see how the children grow up, wondering what will this child be?

Cain murdered his brother thus completing the will of death to take away one of your greatest joys. I feared that you would die from despair, torn by guilt. Not only did you not give in, I believe you finally accepted your own responsibility in our loss of Eden and God has rewarded you with a new son, Seth.

You have become a shining light again for all of us.

You are the one the serpent lives in fear of, Eve. His vigilance will never wane while the earth is under his power. I can only do my best to protect you and our daughters, but I fear the future for our women - the doorways of life and the portals for one who will come and crush his head.

Your loving husband,

Adam

The frustration of existence in a fallen world

My dearest Eve,

My level of frustration was so high today that I was envious of Abel.

Nothing I did today worked, the children were disobedient, the wind and rain relentless. I am cold, tired, and hungry.

Somewhere beyond this world Abel now enjoys an existence where he doesn't have to think about crops being destroyed by storms or taking care of sick animals, or having to look into the faces of his children and tell them there isn't much food...again.

Why does God punish us so harshly for eating one fruit? Who can exist under the weight of such guilt while fighting to feed a family every single day? Is there some kind of pleasure God takes in punishing us that we cannot understand? Was exile from Paradise totally necessary?

When we return – if we return – we will never, ever break such a simple law again.

How long will this go on?

With frustration,

Adam

Graveside letter to Eve

My beloved Eve,

Today the wind is colder, the earth more stubborn, the sky darker, and the animals quiet.

Tears have marked my face and my eyes burn from the long hours I have wept in solitude at your passing, my love. For you and for the children, I fight against the sadness in my heart because there is still work to be done though I secretly long to be with you wherever you are.

These passing days have made me face the truth about what would have happened if we had stayed in Paradise. Death could never have taken you away, to leave a hole in my heart as big as Eden itself.

With piercing clarity I see how necessary it was for God to create you, my helpmate. What would the world be like without you, Woman, and the Mother of all the Living?

Who would I have been without you?

I would still be alone in Paradise, doing whatever it is I would be doing but not the way as when you walked the earth.

Your very presence inspired me like nothing else did, from the first moments of your creation. Even after our expulsion, I enjoyed the light you carried within you which, though diminished by evil, was not completely destroyed because of our sin.

Regardless of your fall from grace, God remained very close to you because He loved you, His last but greatest creation.

He gave you wisdom and grace...you saw with the other eyes residing within the face of beauty upon earth. They perceived things in this world that I would never even have guessed at, for how certain could one be without the insight of the other to whom the world was presented as a gift and a treasure?

You opened my eyes to understand the purpose of God's law without saying a word. Your delicate touch felt more like an angel than a human.

How would I have known the power of God without the only one who was able to bridge Heaven and Earth? What children would have laughed and played at my feet without you, Eve? Or how much could I have loved if you had not taught me about love?

The simplicity of your wisdom, from a little kiss to stop the tears of a child to your cleverness in making do with whatever I could raise from the earth to feed us. Truthfully, God made you as a doorway of life and love and wisdom, didn't He?

In Eden, your footsteps seemed not to touch the earth, your voice would subdue the wind, your gentle requests seemed but the sweetest command to my soul...oh, Eve, Eve...what was Paradise but trees and animals before you came down from heaven!

After life itself, you were my greatest gift.

But for my sins God has taken you back before me and the pain of your loss will simply not go away. I'm certain today that it never will.

My remaining days will not be of peace or light, but suffering solitude, to feel the proper remorse for what I could have given you, Eve, if only I had loved you enough to do what I knew was right.

Whatever that divine gift was we surrendered to the serpent on that horrible day in Eden, I secretly prayed and worked to win it back for you. Not the things of the earth, for you possessed those as much as I did. And not the animals, for they still love you... no, it was the light of God, Himself, dwelling in you as in no other being, not even the angels.

I wanted to give that gift back to you but I couldn't. Only God could do it, and someday he will because he promised.

Sadly, I will have to wait to see you shine like the sun again.

Our youngest, Ada, who is not so young

anymore – she said to me that she dreams of you so often you must still be among us. I had to turn away to hide my tears.

Poor thing, she thought I was angry at her for saying that. I'll have to tell her later that I agree with her, though I wish you were here in body as well. She reminds me so much of you, Eve, I often shake my head to make sure I am not seeing an apparition.

I am so grateful to God for my daughters! Evil hates them so much for one of them – who knows which? – will give birth to his destroyer. I know I must protect them but my days in mortal flesh are coming to an end soon.

I will have to leave them alone for that is the Will of God but they have a piece of your spirit, Eve, and they are clever enough to see behind shadows. I only hope that Cain's violence does not overwhelm the earth and subdue the very being that could bring forth the seed of victory.

Here I kneel by your grave which is beside Abel's, just as you wanted it. Here at least I feel close to you and our dead son; it is my last refuge from the coldness of this world.

I have the memories of you and Paradise, too. They inspire me to see God's hand with the eyes of my soul, though my human eyes cannot.

I was always proud of you, Eve.

All these years have passed and we did

the best we could as a family. We thrived in the face of hateful passion and savage murder. How could that have been possible except for the watchful providence of God and the hope you, my love, never let us abandon of His keeping the promise to you?

Even when I was warned in a dream that you would not recover from this sickness, you wouldn't let us mourn your approaching death because you said the promise of God would be fulfilled in time by one of your daughters.

Thank you for saying that. I will hold those words close to my heart until I die.

This was our world, my love, and the serpent's head will be crushed one day because of Woman.

I know you await me and the rest of the children within the gardens of life.

Your grieving husband,

Adam

Epilogue

Einstein once said that "Imagination is more important than knowledge" so, for the uptight scholars out there who may feel that I've recreated creation, try and relax.

I must admit that I did take some artistic liberties with the preceding letters. It was not my intention to rewrite the creation accounts and I don't believe I have. I just imagined what it could have been like for Adam and Eve.

My next book will really make you wonder about the creation story, though: "The Secrets of Satan". It's about the creation and war among the angels, which precedes the creation of Adam and Eve but is directly related to them.

A special thanks goes out to everyone who helped me to make this book a reality. You know who you are!

God bless.

To my Beloved Eve . . .